Sandy's Suitcase

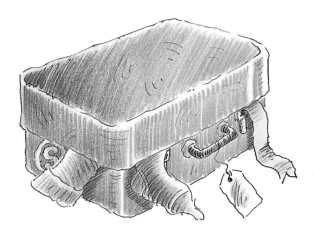

Written by Elsy Edwards
Illustrated by Philip Webb

Sandy opened the small suitcase. In it
were the clothes she had worn last winter.

She dumped out everything. Where she was going, she wouldn't need winter pajamas, or overalls, or her woolen sweater with the flowers on it, or her sweat suit, or her winter party dress.

Instead, she packed the suitcase with everything she would need.

First, a big bottle of apple juice, because she was always thirsty in the desert.

4

Next, she packed a roll of ribbon to tie
around the trees in the scary forest, so
she would know the way back. She
wouldn't get lost this time.

She packed a flashlight, in case the moon
went behind the clouds again, like the
last time.

She put in two bananas for supper, an orange for breakfast, and seven cookies for in-between.

She put in a couple of T-shirts and a spare pair of shorts.

While she was wondering if she needed
anything else, Tiger Cat, the kitten, came
up to see what she was doing.

Tiger Cat tried getting into the suitcase,
but Sandy wouldn't let him.

"Are you leaving home?" asked Sandy's
big sister.

Sandy shook her head.

"Are you going visiting, then?" asked her
big sister.

"No," said Sandy.

'It might be cold at night, when it's dark
and very, very late,' Sandy thought.

So she took out one T-shirt and put in
her fluffy green sweater and her big blue
jacket, instead.

13

She added two books to read, her cuddly bear Mervyn, and her small gray monkey.

Then she put in her recorder, in case she needed some music, some spare socks, in case her feet got wet in the wallowing swamp, and lots of chewing gum.

"Sandy! Where ARE you going?" asked her big sister.

Sandy dragged the suitcase over beside her bed, next to her boots. She closed her eyes and snuggled down under the covers.

"See you in the morning," Sandy said.

Her sister looked confused.

"I'm going to sleep," Sandy said. "No scary dream is going to bother me tonight. I'm ready for anything."

"Oh!" her sister said. "Sweet dreams."

16